THE MILKMAN

THE DELIVERY

JAMES ROBERTS

Edited by

JAMES ROBERTS

Illustrated by

JAMES ROBERTS

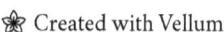 Created with Vellum

I dedicate this book to all those who have been traumatized by a predator and the justice deserved.

CONTENTS

INTRODUCTION

*This book is once again centered around the Harford Police Department
when Officers Bobbie, Richard, Angela, and Amanda, headed by Chief Julia
Lillus, work diligently to solve robberies in the neighborhood and a man with
a certain fetish leading to assault. Clever and ingenious work by the Department cracks the cases with a special twist.*

ANDY AND CLAIRE

"*A*ndy, I have another client who wishes our services inspecting a home she is thinking of purchasing. As usual, I have set the appointment with the homeowner not being present," says Claire.

"I am assuming we are talking about a home in an upscale neighborhood?" asks Andy.

"Andy Robertson, you should know by now I only accept clients who are looking for upscale homes owned by rich owners. You know that is how my business runs!" exclaims Claire.

"And Gus?"

"Andy, your brother is welcome to accompany you, but as always..."

"Yes, I know. Make sure he puts things back where he found them."

"That is correct Andy."

GUS

"Gus, we have another job," says Andy.

"Oh, Andy, is it a female?"

"Gus, I assume a female is the owner or at least part owner of the home."

"Oh boy, I can't wait!" exclaims Gus.

"Now Gus, remember the rules..."

"Yup, put everything back where I found it, except for one souvenir."

"Gus, I don't want you to do what we talked about. Are you clear on that?"

"Andy, I guess so, but I need to do it somehow."

"I will take you over to Dover street. Does that work for you?"

"Well, I guess so, but it isn't the same," says Gus.

THE OFFICE

"Good morning Julia."

"Hi, Bobbie. How are my little darlings?"

"They are fine. Richard will be along shortly. He is finishing up getting the little one ready for school."

"You know, they are growing way too fast," says Julia.

"Yes, I know. It just might be time…"

"Bobby, are you thinking about having another?"

"Well, Richard and I aren't planning for one, but you know Richard. All it takes is catching me off guard."

"And that is hard, Bobbie?"

"Funny Julia, real funny."

"Good morning Amanda," says Julia.

"Hi, Julia. How are you this fine sunny day?"

"Everything is quiet at the moment in Harford," says Julia.

"How is Angela doing with her first pregnancy?" asks Bobbie.

"She is doing fine. She looks like she could be due at any time."

"Amanda, when is she due?" asks Julia.

"Oh, not for another two months."

"And how is her hubby?" asks Bobbie.

"He is on cloud nine with her pregnancy. He is so nice to her. If I were to have a husband, he would be the type I would want," says Amanda.

"There is always hope, Amanda," says Julia.

"Yes, I know, but let's not go there at this moment."

"Good morning Richard," says Julia.

"Did you have any problems with little Richie?" asks Bobbie.

"Oh, not really. He does like to putter around. He just loves the little truck that honks," says Richard.

"Yeah, I know he loves that truck. He gets upset when I tell him he can't take it to school with him," says Bobbie.

"Uh, oh, I guess I goofed that up," says Richard cowardly.

"You, didn't Richard?"

"I am afraid so, Bobbie!"

"I know what that means Richard. You are going to have to make it up to her, you know," states Julia.

"Yeah, I know, but making it up to her is so much pleasure..."

"Here we go again!" exclaims Amanda.

"OK, guys. Did you hear we have a new Real Estate Company that has moved in just outside Harford in the Steinway area," says Julia.

"Yes, I believe the name is Remington Real Estate," says Bobbie.

"Steinway? Isn't that a more upscale neighborhood?" asks Amanda.

"Yes, it is as a matter of fact," says Julia.

THE HOME INSPECTION

"Andy, I am going upstairs to the bedroom," says Gus.

"Remember, Gus, what we discussed."

"Yeah, OK Andy."

"Gus, while you are up there, try to do some inspecting. It will help me a lot," says Andy.

"Oh my, pink, red, black, and oh, beige. Such a beautiful aroma. I think I will take this one," says Gus to himself.

"Are you OK up there, Gus?"

"Sure thing Andy, I am in heaven. Her name is Rebecca Stone and she is beautiful!"

"Finish up there. We are almost done here," says Andy.

"Look here, Andy. Here is my souvenir," says Gus.

"Great Gus. I have found many items Claire will be happy to learn about."

"When do we do it, Andy?"

"Probably not for a few days. Claire will tell us."

REBECCA STONE

"*P*aul, you must not stay. Rob will be home soon and the last thing we need is for him to walk in on us," says Rebecca.

"Oh, don't fret, Becky. One more "toss in the hay" as they say?"

"Paul, come over here and get it done!"

"So, you and Rob are selling the house?"

"Yes, Paul. We are moving to Cleveland in a much bigger house."

"Becky, does that mean we are done?"

"No way, Paul! There is no way I am going to stop our interludes."

"You are being careful. Rob doesn't suspect?"

"No, he is so busy with his job, he hardly has time for me, let alone to get fucked by him."

"Well Becky, I am satisfying you?"

"Yes, Paul. Hurry up and let's get it on before I get all dried out."

"I can fix that quickly…"

"I love when you do that to me Paul…"

CLAIRE REMINGTON

"Andy, what did you find at the Stone's residence?"

"Here is the list, Claire. They are quite rich and there are many things in there that will bring top dollar."

"Great! Now get busy and write up that inspection report. If you write up the report so my client is satisfied and I get a sale, you will get the typical five percent."

"And what about the revenue from the contents?"

"Andy, you know I also compensate you."

"Are you sure you don't want me in on the break-in, Claire?"

"No Andy, I can't have you involved in that capacity. I need you to not be tied into the operation. That is why I have set this company up in the way that I have. In case anything goes wrong, I need a safety net to make sure I get little collateral damage and still have most of my people to continue."

"Gus is really falling for the Stone woman," says Andy.

"Yes, I knew that would happen. It happens all the time. Just be sure he does not get in the way. Remind him that he can look all he wants, but he must not ever touch," says Claire.

GUS INVESTIGATES

"Hey Andy. You know that Rebecca Stone?"

"Yes, Gus, what have you searched for now? You always get right to the Internet after an inspection when you accompany me."

"Well, Andy, she has a lover!"

"Oh, how do you know that?"

"Look right here."

"I'll be darned, Gus. It appears you are correct."

"Andy, you know what that means? Gus, you have to be careful. If Claire ever were to find out about this, it would be all over for me and I don't know what she would do to both of us. You know she has connections we know nothing about."

"Andy, I am always careful. The 'milkman' always leaves his mark undetected."

TRAFFIC VIOLATIONS AND A HOOKER

"*J*ulia, all I have for today is a bunch of traffic tickets," says Richard.

"That is good news. I don't mind those types of violations. It is those other cases we get into that worry me."

"And who is she, Richard?" asks Bobbie.

"Well, she is what you call 'a woman of the streets'."

"Oh, you mean a hooker. Where did you find her? Dover street?"

"Yes, Bobbie, she tried to proposition me while I was writing a ticket."

"You propositioned him while he was in uniform and writing a ticket?" asks Bobbie.

"Oh, yes, I thought he couldn't resist me..."

"Resist you, sister? He has something much better at home than anything you can offer..."

"OK, OK, let's cut to the chase," interjects Julia.

"Look, I am new at this. I don't have a place to stay, and I don't have money...," says the hooker.

"Look, sweetheart, you and I are going to have a little chat about this and when we are done, I am sure you will be re-thinking your so-called occupation," says Julia.

9

"Uh, oh. Julia is going to be giving her the 'why the hell are you selling your body' speech," says Bobbie.

"I feel sorry for her," says Richard.

"Richard, were you at the least interested in her proposition? What did she do?" asks Bobbie.

"Oh, nothing much. I figured she was new at it..."

"Why, Richard?"

"Calm down Bobbie. She came up to me and, well the pants she..."

"You mean 'Hot Pants™'?"

"Well, yes. Those pants have a zipper in the front and she..."

"What did she do Richard?"

"Well, she started unzipping them in front of me."

"Oh, and what did you see?"

"Nothing much. I didn't look..."

"Nothing much?"

"Well, just some pubic hair...."

"OK, enough Richard!"

"But, Bobbie, you kept asking me..."

"You two..." says Amanda shaking her head.

THE VISIT TO REBECCA STONE

"Who is there?"

"It's the 'milkman'."

"The 'milkman'! I didn't order any milk, and they don't do that anymore, do they?"

"You are Rebecca, correct?"

"Yes."

"And you are? What do you want?"

"Becky is it?"

"Why are you calling me Becky?"

"Well, that is what Paul calls you, isn't it?"

"How do you know about Paul?"

"I know a lot about you and Paul, and what you are wearing…pink, black, today?"

"Look, I don't know who you are, but I need you to leave!"

"I told you I am the 'milkman'."

"Please leave!"

"Not so fast, unless you want your husband to know about Paul and…"

"What do you want from me?"

"What color panties are you wearing? Pink, red, or your black ones? Maybe the beige?"

"How do you know about my panties?"

"Oh, I know a lot about your panties and their aroma."

"You are sick!"

"Look, I actually have a red pair of yours and…"

"How did you get those?"

"It doesn't matter. What matters is that you take your panties off and hand them over to me."

"No, I won't do it!"

"So, let me see, Rob's number, yes, I have it on my phone…"

"Wait, please don't call him."

"OK, so take off your panties and hand them over to me and while you have them off, let's get down to it."

"What do you mean?"

"I want to smell you…your panties and then I am going to fuck you."

"No, I will give you my panties, but I won't let you…"

"Rob's phone is ringing…"

"No, please. Hang up. I will do what you want."

"Look, it shouldn't be that difficult for you. You spread those legs for Paul and Rob, so just spread them for me."

"Just get it over with and leave me alone!"

"Good, now get over to that table there and bend over…"

DOVER STREET

"Gus, do you want me to take you over to Dover Street? It has been a few days since we were at the Stone's home," says Andy.

"No, I think I am all set."

"Gus that isn't like you..."

"Really Andy, I am OK."

"Are you sure, Gus?"

"Look Andy, I have another pair of Becky's panties. Would you like to smell them? They are sure her..."

"Gus, I told you before. I am not like you. I don't have the panty sniffing fetish. I allow you to act it out, and that is it, so put those panties away. By the way where did you get those beige panties? Are they Rebecca Stone's?"

THE STONE RESIDENCE

"*H*ello, is this the Harford Police Department?"

"Yes, it is. I am Julia the Police Chief and who am I speaking with?"

"My name is Rebecca Stone and I am calling to report a robbery. You see, my husband and I are selling our home and today when I got home many of my belongings are missing."

"What sort of items are missing, Ms. Stone?"

"Our home is furnished with some quite expensive items and I have jewelry worth quite a bit of money. Those high price items are missing."

"When did this robbery take place?"

"Ms. Julia, I really don't know. I was out of town for a couple of days."

"It is just Julia. Where was your husband?"

"He also was out of town with business.

"Was there any damage done to your home, such as in breaking in, Ms. Stone?"

"No, nothing is broken. My front door was even locked when I arrived. I don't know how anyone actually got in."

"You say you are selling your home. Has there been anyone in your

14

home lately for the selling transaction like a home inspection, a realtor…?"

"I did have a home inspection done, but that was a few weeks ago. I have had a couple meetings with the realtor….and Oh, a guy came to my door the other day…"

"What did this guy want?"

"Oh, he was looking for someone and got the wrong house. He looked way too innocent to be a robber."

"Ms. Stone, you never know. Is it OK if I send an Officer over to your home to check further for clues?"

"Yes, Julia. I am home now and will be for the next couple of days."

"OK, an Officer will be over to visit tomorrow. His name is Richard Peltz."

THE VISIT TO ELIZABETH PENDLETON

"Mrs. Pendleton, it is the 'milkman'."

"'Milkman'? There isn't any milkmen anymore."

"I think you might want to let me in Lizzy, I have important information."

"What is with calling me Lizzy? Only..."

"Oh, only Patrick calls you Lizzy."

"How do you know about Pat?"

"Look, what color are you wearing? Black, Pink..."

"What are you talking about?"

"What color panties are you wearing?"

"What is the matter with you..."

"Look here, do you recognize these?"

"Those look like my..."

"Yes, you are correct, these are your lace panties and oh, do they smell so good..."

"How did you get those? I found I was missing those."

"It doesn't matter. I want you to remove your panties and hand them over to me."

"What! Are you sick?"

"Look here, I have Joe's phone number right here on my phone. I can dial it…"

"No, please! He doesn't know about Pat."

"He doesn't need to know about what you and Pat are up to, and I won't tell him as long as you do as I ask. Now remove your panties!"

"Here, you sick bastard!"

"Oh, you have such a sweet aroma. Let's see if I can get right up close to it…"

"What are you talking about?"

"Now you have your panties off, I am going to fuck you!"

"There is no way you are going to do that to me!"

"Lizzy, Joe's phone is ringing…"

"No, no, please. I will do it."

"That is better. Tell you what, I will give you a choice. Shall we go into your bedroom and use your bed, or would you just rather bend over the back of this couch?"

"Just get it over with and get the hell out of my house!"

"All right! Bend over here and lift your skirt…"

ANDY IS CONFUSED

"Gus, why is it you don't want to go to Dover Street after all the inspections? We have had a few lately and never once have you wanted to go to Dover Street."

"Andy, I swear, I am good. Don't worry, I will go again."

"You know, Gus, your hand is not like the real thing. You should know that."

"Andy, I am fine. If you want me to go to Dover Street, I will."

"Another thing, Gus, since when have you started stealing two pairs of panties?"

"I don't know. I don't always take two pairs of panties, just with a few homes."

"What makes the decision whether you take one pair or two pair of panties, Gus?"

"I don't know…maybe it is how beautiful I feel she is or maybe the aroma…"

"So, let me get this straight. You take one pair of panties from all the women, but some you take two pairs, depending on beauty and the smell of them?"

'Yeah, Andy, something like that…"

MRS. PENDELTON

"Hello, yes, this is Julia the Police Chief of the Harford Police Department. How may I help you?"

"Yes, Ms. Julia..."

"Julia."

"Yes, Julia, my house has been robbed. I was out of town a couple of days and when I got home, things were missing."

"Are there any signs of the break-in, Ms. Pendleton?"

"No, none. The doors were all locked."

"Was your husband home? Oh, excuse me, I am presuming you are married."

"Yes, Julia, I am married and no, he was out of town as well."

"Have you had any visitors, strangers in your home lately?"

'We are selling our home, so we had a home inspector here and some guy knocked on my door."

"What did this guy want?"

"He mistook me for someone else."

"Did he look innocent?"

"Oh, yes. I wouldn't suspect him at all."

"What about the home inspector?"

"He was here. He is appointed by my Realtor."

"Who is your Realtor?"

"It is the Remington Real Estate Company."

"Ms. Pendleton, may I ask the type of items taken from your home?"

"We are quite rich, so high price items and jewelry."

"Is it OK if we send an Officer over to inspect your home to determine how someone was able to enter your home?"

"Yes, Julia. How about tomorrow at around noon?"

"That will be fine, Mrs. Pendleton."

THE OFFICE CONFERENCE

"*R*ichard is there anything to compare with the houses reported to have been robbed?" asks Julia.

"Whoever broke into the homes is very sophisticated in their method and it appears that because of this, every home robbed was probably robbed by the same person or group of people."

"Please explain, Richard."

"OK, Julia. There were no windows broken or doors broken into. It appears that the door locks were picked. I could find no finger-prints, no broken items in the homes. The items left are considered valuable or high priced, but it then appears what was taken had a much higher value. It appears these robberies were very well planned and tuned to exactly the type items they wanted."

"So, we are looking at a very professional operation?" asks Bobbie.

"Yes, it appears so," says Richard.

"So, let's talk about the similarities," says Julia.

"I have that tallied, Julia," says Amanda.

"OK, Bobbie, please put those similarities up on the screen," says Julia.

"All the homes reported robbed were for sale and under contract with the Remington Real Estate Company. All the homes were inspected under contract with the Real Estate Company, and we might assume at this point the home inspection company is the same. Is that all of the similarities, Amanda?" asks Julia.

"There is one more thing that is similar and strange at the same time. Every one of the women who called and reported the robbery mentioned a stranger knocking on their door and supposedly, what they told us, was looking for someone other than the women's door he knocked on. Also, each woman mentioned that this stranger was very innocent looking and either said they didn't suspect him as the robber or that they insinuated this with the tone of voice displayed to us."

"It almost sounds as if they are hiding something or afraid of something," says Bobbie.

"What do we know about these women?" asks Julia.

"I looked into this a little, but my findings are not conclusive, but there is a very good chance that at least one or more of them are involved in some kind of affair," says Richard.

"Do you mean an extramarital affair, Richard?" asks Bobbie.

"Yes."

"Hmm," says Bobbie.

"Richard, I would like you to go over to the Remington Real Estate Company and see if you can get any information from them that might put some of this together. Amanda, I would like you to go and talk with these women and see what information you can get to these supposed affairs. There may be a connection. Bobbie, you and I will scout out the home inspection company once Richard gets that information. And then, I am going to visit my god children," says Julia.

THE REMINGTON REAL ESTATE COMPANY

"Hello, my name is Officer Richard Peltz and I would like to speak with the CEO of this company."

"Please hold on. Ms. Remington there is an Officer Peltz wishing to speak with you."

"Let him in."

"Hello, my name is Officer Richard Peltz and I would like to speak with you pertaining to some of the Real Estate transactions recently."

"Certainly. My name is Claire. What can I help you with?"

"I am certain you have heard about the robberies involving a few of the homes selling under contract with your company?"

"Yes, I have, and I must say I am very sorry for my clients and at the same time concerned."

"Concerned, Ms. Remington?"

"Yes, I can't help to think that these robberies might paint a shadow over my company."

"Yes, I understand, but what I am here for is to see if you can shed some light on these robberies, like who is the home inspector under contract? Not that I am suspecting, but I am sure you realize I have to cover all bases."

"Yes, I understand completely, and I have nothing to hide as far as

23

the home inspector under contract. His name is Andy Robertson whose company is the same. I have had him under contract for at least three years."

"Ms. Remington, does your contracted home inspector inspect the homes while your client is at home?"

"Most of the time, no. You see, my company focuses heavily on the upper end of the home buying and selling niche. Therefore, our clients are terribly busy with their businesses and life and are not usually present during the home inspection."

"Do any of your clients ever object on having a home inspection without them being present?"

"No. Never have we had any objections or complaints."

"Do you trust your contracted home inspector?"

"Yes, very much so. I never doubt his expertise and never would believe he would be involved in robberies. I am sorry, Officer Peltz, but looking at my company and my contractors for answers to the robberies, we have none and definitely not involved."

"Thank you, Ms. Remington. I appreciate your time and thank you for the information you have given to me."

AMANDA DISCOVERS THE MILKMAN

"Mrs. Stone, my name is Officer Amanda Alexandria, and I would like to speak with you for a moment if I can."

"Yes, please come in. Would you like a cup of tea?"

"Yes, please."

"What can I help you with, Officer Alexandria?"

"Please call me Amanda."

"Amanda what is it I can help you with?"

"We are aware of the robbery that occurred at your home here, but my visit is to discuss with you about the stranger who knocked on your door and mistook you for someone else he was looking for."

"Yes, a very confused man."

"Confused? How so, Mrs. Stone?"

"Well, he acted sheepishly and was very apologetic about disturbing me with his mistaken identity."

"Did he give a name?"

"No, he did not….wait a minute, he mentioned something like he introduced himself as the 'milkman'."

"The 'milkman'? Was he or did he look like he was selling milk? Who does that nowadays?"

"No, he did not appear to even look like a 'milkman' should look and he didn't have any milk to sell to me. He didn't even try to sell milk to me."

"Mrs. Stone, what did he try to sell to you?"

"Amanda, I don't know what you mean?"

"Mrs. Stone let me ask you, and I am trying to level with you. What happened with the 'milkman'?"

"Nothing. He just wanted...I..."

"He wanted what, Mrs. Stone."

"He just mistook me for another person..."

"Mrs. Stone. I am here to help. I believe there is more that you need to tell me."

"Amanda, I can't...I just can't..."

"Look, I see tears in your eyes. There is something more than just mistaken identity."

"Amanda, what I have to tell you cannot be spoken outside of this conversation."

"Mrs. Stone, you do realize the Police Department must be involved with all facets of a case, but I can assure you that the Department is where it stops. You can trust me...and us."

"Amanda, I am married, and my husband is so busy with his business.... I, I, well, I have a guy that I am having an affair with...I am so embarrassed."

"Go ahead. I am not judgmental."

"Well, the 'milkman', well, he....oh, this is so tough..."

"Take your time..."

"I do not know how he got this information..."

"What information is that?"

"He knew I was having an affair. He knew the name of him, and he knew the name of my husband."

"So, he was setting you up with blackmail?"

"Yes, if I did not do what he asked, then he was going to tell my husband. He actually had his phone number and started dialing..."

"What did he want you to do, Mrs. Stone?"

"Please don't think ill of me...you see I had to do it, I, I cannot afford to end this affair..."

"I am not judging…"

"He told me to remove my panties and that he was going to have sexual relations with me."

"So, you did…"

"He also had a pair of my panties with him besides the ones I was wearing that I took off and threw at him. He was so disgusting…"

"How so?"

"After I removed my panties and threw them at him, he immediately took them to his nose and sniffed the crotch area…"

"How do you think he got a pair of your panties?"

"I have no idea. It really scares me."

"What happened next?"

"To put it bluntly, he forced me to bend over my table and he fucked me!"

THE ANDY ROBERTSON HOME INSPECTION COMPANY

"Hello, Andy is it?"

"Yes."

"I am Police Chief Julia Lillus and this is Officer Bobbie Pelz of the Harford Police Department. We are here to speak with you about your contract with the Remington Real Estate Company. You are contracted to them for home inspections?"

"Yes, Officers, we exclusively perform home inspections for their clients."

"You say we?" Do you have a partner?"

"No. I am the only person in my company."

"So, you do the home inspections on your own and are the clients present when performing your home inspections?"

"No, hardly ever are they present. You see, her clients are at the upper end of the pay scale. They don't have the time or really want to be present."

"So, they are not present, and you are totally on your own throughout the whole process?" asks Bobbie.

"Yes, that is correct."

"You mentioned 'her'. Who is 'her'?" asks Julia.

"Oh, she, Claire Remington, is who I am contracted with. She is the owner of Remington Real Estate."

"I see. So, tell me. These clients are at the upper end of the pay scale, as you say, you must encounter may expensive items within these homes?" asks Julia.

"That is correct Chief Lillus."

"Julia, if you don't mind."

"Yes, Julia, that is correct. I have to be incredibly careful to not accidentally bump something and break it."

"Andy, have you heard about the robberies in some of the homes you actually inspected?"

"Yes, Claire had mentioned it to me."

"Expensive items, jewelry. Wouldn't you agree it would be quite easy to take some of those items, especially if I were totally alone in the home?"

"Officer Peltz, I hope you are not suggesting that I had anything to do with those robberies!"

"No, not at all. I was just wondering if you might agree…just the situation," says Bobbie.

"Yes, I suppose it would be reasonably easy."

"Thank you for taking the time to speak with us, Andy," says Julia.

"My pleasure Chief and Officer Peltz. If I can be of any further help, you know where I am."

QUESTIONING ELIZABETH PENDELTON

"*M*rs. Pendleton, why do you think this stranger knocked on your door?" asks Amanda.

"He said he mistook me for someone else."

"Did he tell you his name?"

"No, he just apologized and left."

"Mrs. Pendleton just suppose someone was involved in something that they didn't want someone else to know about. Could that result in blackmail?"

"Yes, I suppose it could."

"Could it make that person do just about anything to hide that secret?"

"Yes, Amanda, I am sure they probably would."

"Mrs. Pendleton, why the tears? Who did he say he was?"

"He did...he, he…..he said he was the 'milkman'…"

"Was he selling milk to you?"

"No, I didn't think milkmen still existed..."

"So, what was the blackmail, Mrs. Pendleton?"

"Well, I, I…"

"An affair, Mrs. Pendleton?"

"Yes, yes...an affair...I am sorry…"

"I am not judging you."

"He…well…he told me to take my panties off and give them to him. When I gave them to him he immediately put the crotch to his nose and took a deep breath…"

"He threatened to call my husband right then, if I did not cooperate."

"What happened next Mrs. Pendleton?"

"Well, he forced me over to my couch and pushed me over the back…"

"Then what?"

"I, I, oh, I don't want to say…the sick bastard…"

"It is OK, Mrs. Pendleton, I am listening and not judgmental."

"He ordered me to…to…to lift my skirt and then he fucked me…he fucked me hard. I don't think he was wearing any protection….I could feel it…I could…"

"That is all right Mrs. Pendleton."

"Amanda, he fucked me!" exclaims Mrs. Pendleton as the tears turn into a dosing over her cheeks.

"One last thing Mrs. Pendleton. Did he have a pair of your panties besides the one pair you took off for him?"

"Yes, he did. I don't know how he got them…"

PUTTING IT ALL TOGETHER MAKING NO SENSE

"OK everyone, let's chart what we have learned," says Julia. "Richard?"

"I met with a Claire Remington the owner of the Remington Real Estate Company involved with clients at the upper end of the pay scale, meaning fairly rich. She contracts a home inspection company to aid her clients."

"Bobbie?"

"Julia and I met with the Andy Home Inspection Company, who as Richard says, contracts to the Remington Real Estate Company to perform home inspections to their clients. The home inspections are done mainly without the client being present."

"Amanda?"

"It asked some open-ended questions, but I got some interesting information and the truth about this stranger who supposedly knocked on their doors claiming mistaken identification. It turns out, just as Bobbie surmised, each of those women are involved in an affair. This stranger named himself as the 'milkman'. He blackmailed them, threatening to call their husbands right on the spot if they did not do what he wanted. So, he forced them to remove their panties and then raped them. Funny thing is this 'milkman' turns out to be a panty sniffer and he had, in all cases, a pair of their panties besides the one he forced them to remove."

"How kinky and sick!" exclaims Bobbie.

"Well, I looked up panty sniffing, and it is a fetish predominantly done by the male gender. It is important for the person with this fetish to smell the crotch area of a pair of female panties," says Amanda.

"Oh, how gross!" exclaims Bobbie.

"Bobbie, that turns you off?" asks Richard.

"Richard, it turns me off if a guy is doing that to panties that do not belong to his wife!"

"Oh, OK, I was getting a little worried...," says Richard.

"Ah hem, OK, Amanda, do you have anything else to report?" asks Julia.

"Yes, I was trying to understand the 'milkman' stigma that this stranger was claiming to be. I found out that a person that handles/pleases the wifey /girlfriend when the husband or boyfriend is away. You heard the saying *'That baby doesn't look anything like you. Better ask the wife about the 'milkman'.'*"

"I see the correlation, he is calling himself the 'milkman' because of the definition you just gave, but also in the act he is transferring his..."

"Richard, I am not sure if that is supposed to be in the definition," says Bobbie.

"Well, it is white, isn't it?"

"Richard, don't be so gross!"

"I am not being gross. I am the 'milkman'..."

"Richard!"

"Bobbie, I don't mean the first part of the definition. I am referring to the...."

"Yes, Richard, we all know what you are referring to," says Julia.

"Poor Bobbie," says Amanda under her breath.

"The question I have is how did he get the other pair of panties he arrived with when he knocked at the door of these women?" asks Julia.

"He would have had to get into their houses and in their bedroom dressers at some time," says Bobbie.

"Could he be the robber?" asks Amanda.

"I am thinking not," says Julia.

"Why do you say that Julia?" asks Richard.

"Because I think a person with the panty sniffing fetish that is so intense to move them into the act of vaginal intercourse doesn't have the capacity to think about anything else. To put it bluntly, all he really wants is some pussy!"

"So, what about the home inspector?" asks Bobbie.

"I didn't get the feeling he had the sophistication to pull off a robbery so precise to leave no traces," says Julia.

"It appears we actually have two situations. A robbery and a 'milkman' running around sniffing panties and raping," says Richard.

"Wait a minute. I know what you guys are thinking!" exclaims Amanda.

"Well, she is married to a higher class of husband and she lives in that neighborhood with that kind of home," says Bobbie.

"But she is pregnant, you know," says Amanda.

"Look, we have used her before, and she does a great job with the roles we have given her. She has told me she wants to come and work," says Julia.

"Look, one of us can be in her home with her at all times; she can fake meaning to sell her home and select the Remington Company for the real estate needs. We can be there for the home inspection, covertly of course. We can see if the panty sniffer is in any relation to this hunch of ours. I can hire Betsy to be the purchasing person wishing to buy Angela's home. Here is the tricky part, Richard, I will use you for her lover…"

"Wait a minute, Julia…!" exclaims Bobbie.

"No, no, not in realty. He will not even be with her at any time. I will use his name and position as an Officer. We have at our disposal a very high-tech geek who can set up an information search page that will pop-up when the 'milkman' performs a search, assuming that is where he is getting his information for women who are having affairs, but I am sure he never finds that information anyways. I think he just takes his chances on women hoping they are having an affair so he can force them through blackmail. I wonder though, how he has been so accurate with just luck. I know there is some connection between the 'milkman', the home inspector and the robberies," says Julia.

ANGELA

"*H*ello, Angela! It is so good to see you. How is that bundle of joy?" asks Bobbie.

"It sure is nice to be here again and see all of you. As you can see, this bundle of joy is invading my belly," answers Angela.

"Angela, we have a job for you, if you are up to it and it is in line with your doctor's orders," says Julia.

"Oh, yes. I miss all of you so much and I sure miss my work," says Angela.

"What we have is a span of robberies in homes that are being sold; a stranger who sniffs panties and may also be involved with rape," says Julia.

"Oh my, I am sure not up to working a rape case," says Angela.

"You won't be in any danger of that, Angela," says Julia.

"You and your husband will be selling your home in this set up with a specific Real Estate Company we think may be involved in the robberies. Because it appears the robberies are with upscale living, we will be adding some, should we say, high priced items in your home and high priced jewelry. Don't worry, these items really are not the real thing. There is a home inspection company that is contracted with this Realtor and we think he may be the connection to which homes to rob," says Bobbie.

"We are not sure where the panty sniffing guy fits in if he even does, but we will be setup for him if he shows up. You won't be in danger because Richard will be in your home, covertly, at all times ready for anything that may become a danger to you or your husband. So, this is what we are going to be doing to try and lure our sniffer boy," says Julia.

THE LURE

"Charlie, I want you to meet one of our Officers, Angela Simons (Alexandria)," says Julia.

"Oh, hi, Angela. You must be the sister to Amanda. I have been waiting to meet you. I must say beauty has flourished for the both of you," says Charlie.

"OK, so somehow this guy they call the 'milkman'..."

"'Milkman' Julia? asks Angela.

"Yes, honey, I will discuss that with you later."

"So, what is this 'milkman's' gig?" asks Charlie.

"Somehow the 'milkman' gets into one of the upscale homes being sold and takes a pair of panties belonging to the woman of the house. This appears to happen when the homeowners are not at home. At some time later, he again shows up at the homes he has stolen the panties from and confronts the woman of the household. He forces her to have sexual relations with him, rape, with a blackmail scheme. There is some connection to these women having extramarital affairs in the blackmail scheme; threatening to tell their husbands. How he gets this information is beyond me. It appears he might find that information on the Internet somehow. What I need from you, Charlie, is to make a search page showing Angela's secretive affair with

Richard. I want to make it enticing with an Officer of the Police Department," says Julia.

"Well, Julia, you picked Richard for this? Knowing Richard, he will gloat in playing the part!" exclaims Angela.

"Yeah, well it is only in print," says Julia.

"So, you want me to put this search page up complete with Angela's address and the particulars?" asks Charlie.

"Yes, and make sure it pops up first if the 'milkman' does actually search the Internet for information about the women he can blackmail," says Julia.

"Richard will be there to stop him from attacking me?" asks Angela.

"Yes, Richard has been ordered to stay at your home covertly throughout this entire process. There will be no danger to you, and oh, by the way, we will load your dresser with panties that are not belonging to you," says Julia.

"That is good. Panty sniffing freaks me out. I mean you know in a marriage..."

"Yes, Angela, I know what you are referring to," says Julia.

CLAIRE MEETS WITH ANDY

"*A*ndy, I have been visited by the Harford Police Department pertaining to the robberies," says Claire.

"Yes, they paid me a visit too," says Andy.

"Andy, I am going to be laying low for some time."

"You mean no more home sales?"

"No, I don't mean that. What I mean is I will continue acting as a Realtor Company as usual. I will still have you inspect the houses, but there will be no robberies."

"How long is that going to be?"

"I am not sure Andy. I need to get the Police Department off of my back."

"You might want to make sure your panty sniffing brother does not accompany you on the inspections. I never wanted that to happen anyway, and this would be a good time to end it."

"Do you really think his fetish is a danger to your business? We haven't had any complaints from any of the women that a pair of panties was missing from their dresser drawers."

"Andy, I just don't like it! Me, being a woman, cringe just thinking about someone stealing a pair of my panties just to sniff them. It is very disgusting! Put a stop to it Andy!"

GUS IS DISAPPOINTED

"Gus, Claire wants me to put a stop to you going along with me on my home inspections to steal panties."

"What for, Andy? I am not hurting anyone. You know what happens when I can't get some panties. You don't want me to get them the way I used too, do you?"

"Look Gus, I will take you to Dover Street everyday if I need to."

"I don't need any of those bitches on Dover Street as long as I can go with you."

"Gus, you confuse me. I thought your fetish makes you horney as hell!"

"It does!"

"Well, then, how are you satiating your need for some pussy?"

"I have my ways, Andy."

"You don't want to explain, Gus?"

"No. Just know, I have my ways."

"Andy can't I slowly get weaned off not going with you on your inspections? Claire doesn't need to know."

"No, Gus, I don't think so."

ANGELA AND HER HUSBAND ARE SELLING THEIR HOME

"*H*ello Angela and this must be your husband?" asks Claire.

"Yes, hi, this is my husband Robert," answers Angela.

"So, you are in the market in selling your home? Do you have your eye on a home to purchase at this time?"

"Yes, Mrs. Remington..."

"Just call me Claire..."

"Claire, we have our eye on a home over in the Cleveland area."

"Ah, yes. That is a very upscale and wonderful neighborhood. You have come to me at the right time. I have a whole list of people who are interested in purchasing homes such as yours."

"That sounds nice. It means you won't have much difficulty in selling our home?"

"It shouldn't as long as your home is in the condition you have indicated. Of course, there will need to be a home inspection. Most all my purchasing clients want a home inspection. You know, they want to be sure they are getting what is listed, here, on paper."

"We understand."

"You needn't worry about hiring a home inspector because I take care of that for you. It saves you money and the business that contracts to me is very professional and thorough. I have never had a complaint about a home inspection from this company."

"That would be fine with Robert and I."

"Now, I can get the home inspector in this Thursday if that works for you."

"Well, neither Robert or I will be able to be at our home because he is going out of town on business, and I have a couple of doctor's appointments with this belly of mine."

"Oh yes you poor darling. When are you due?"

"Not for a couple of months."

"It must be such an exciting time for you and Robert. A new baby and a new home."

"Can the home inspector do what he needs to do when we are not at home?"

"Yes Angela. Most of my clients are not home during the inspection. People are so busy now-a-days. OK, Thursday will get the ball rolling and I am sure your home will sell fast and for the price you are asking."

HOW DOES GUS DO IT?

"Sid, this is Gus. I have another address for you to do a search on."

"OK, Gus, where is it this time?"

"There is a home being sold on Stafford Street."

"Ok, let me look. Wow, it popped up quickly. Is the house number 2245?"

"Yes, that is it."

"It definitely is an upscale home, Gus."

"What can you tell me about the owners?"

"I can get you that information, but it will cost you. It is getting extremely harder to drill down for that information."

"You know I am good for it, Sid."

"OK, are you ready for this?"

"Yes, shoot."

"The owners of that home are Angela and Robert Simons. She is twenty-eight years old and he is thirty years old. Her maiden name is Alexandria."

"Nice, sweet and young…"

"What was that Gus?"

"Oh, nothing. What else do you have on her?"

"Hang on. This is where it gets difficult. Let me see, I will search Angela Simons and her maiden name Alexandria."

"She isn't a cop, is she?"

"No, not that I can see. Why do you ask?"

"Oh, just wondering, Sid."

"Hey, hey, here we go. I found an Angela Simons with a maiden name Alexandria with a Richard…"

"What do you mean with Richard, Sid?"

"Hang on….here we go…Richard is a Police Officer…"

"What Department, Sid?"

"It does not say, Gus."

"Are they having an affair?"

"Well, Gus, hang on! I don't know why you are so interested in these women and whether they are having an affair."

"It is complicated, Sid. Let us just say I need that information for my investigative purposes."

"Oh, yeah, I forgot about your investigative services. Let me search this Richard…Oh, here it is. It appears Richard is having an affair with Angela. I actually have some pictures of them together and by the looks of it….oh, here it is….Richard and Angela are sharing a kiss."

JULIA IS NERVOUS

"Charlie are you sure that a search on Angela and Richard will show the affair and not that he or she is in the Harford Police Department?" asks Julia.

"Julia don't be so paranoid. Go ahead and search to your hearts content. You will only get what you are looking for and they will only get what you see."

"Oh, Charlie, what is with his photo of Angela and Richard kissing?"

"Photoshop, my dear."

"Bobbie better not see this. Poor Angela…she better not see this either."

"Julia, there is no way that anyone can get anything different than these search results."

"It is amazing, Charlie, how you can do this."

"Would you like me to make a search page for you, Julia?"

"Not a chance! You better not have me kissing any man, especially Richard."

"I could photoshop you kissing me…"

"Charlie! You have way too much time on your hands. I will talk to you later."

AMANDA PURCHASES A HOME

"*H*ello, my name is Amanda Jones. I am looking to purchase a home. It must be upscale and in the Stafford area."

"Well, you have come to Remington Real Estate at the right time. I just listed a beautiful home at 2245 Stafford Street. It is owned by a young couple with no children, yet. It just happens she is pregnant. As a matter of fact, you and her look remarkably similar," says Claire.

"Yes, I get that all the time. Many people think I look like someone they know. I think I look like everybody," says Amanda laughingly.

"Would you like me to take you over to the home for a walk-thru?" asks Claire.

"No, I have seen the photos you have done such a great job with and there is everything I am looking for in a home," says Amanda.

"The home is having a home inspection done Thursday," says Claire.

"Great, I will be happy to see it. I would like to make an offer on the home," says Amanda.

"Well, OK," says Claire surprised.

"They are asking two hundred eighty thousand?" asks Amanda.

"Yes, but I am sure they would take a reasonable reduction. They are in a hurry to sell," says Claire.

"No, I will give them the asking price. I want that house! Go ahead and write up the contract. I will be paying cash."

"Certainly, Amanda. Once all the required paperwork is written up and you have had the chance to read over the inspection report we will set the closing date," says Claire.

"Thank you. I will check back with you next week," says Amanda.

THE RENDEVOUIZ

"$\mathcal{A}$manda were you able to make the purchase of Angela's home," asks Julia.

"Yes Julia. I am hoping my approach didn't spook her."

"I doubt it. We just had to be sure no one else tried to complete a purchase on their home, in that this whole charade is a mock-up."

"Julia, Richard should be back soon. Angela and Robert are still away. I told them not to return to their home until I give them the OK," says Bobbie.

"Richard, how did it go?" asks Julia.

"The home inspector showed up with no one else. It appeared to be the typical inspection and he was not taking any notes on the high-priced items we planted. While he was in the basement, I moved up into Angela and Roberts bedroom, shimmying under the bed. Lucky I am skinny…that bed is quite low to the floor. Anyway, the inspector did not take any underwear or even open any of the dresser drawers. Everything he did appeared to be the up-and-up."

"Ok, now the second part of the plan. Go back Richard and wait and see if there will be a robbery," says Julia.

ANDY CONFRONTS GUS

"Gus, where have you been?" asks Andy.

"Oh, just out."

"Where did you get those panties hanging out of your pocket?"

"At the last inspection I went to. You don't recognize them?"

"I don't know, I don't pay attention to the panties you take."

"Well, these are special. I think they just might become my favorite."

"Gus, have you seen my lock picking tools?"

"No, Andy. Didn't you just use them on the inspection you did yesterday?"

"No, I didn't need them."

"Haven't seen them," says Gus.

"Andy, I think I want to spend some time at Dover Street. Maybe for a few days."

"OK, I will take you there. Just give me a call when you want to come back."

THE HOOKER

"*H*ey, here comes the 'milkman', girls."

"Hey 'milkman', are you here to make a delivery?"

"I'll be here for a while. I am sure I can make a delivery to each one of you, but first I want to see Shirley," says Gus.

"She is up there; second floor."

"Hey, Shirley, it's the 'milkman'."

"How are you Gus?"

"I am doing fine."

"How long are you here for?"

"Well, according to the girls, I have to make a delivery to each one of them. It could take a couple of days."

"My delivery is first!"

"Yes, Shirley, always!"

"Here, I am sure you will want these."

"Have you been wearing them?"

"I just took them off just before you arrived."

"Um..Umm...I can tell they belong to you Shirley."

"Let's get to it Gus. Make your delivery!"

"Gladly, Shirley."

"That was a good delivery, 'milkman'. Have you been holding it just for me?"

"Shirley, you know I always deliver a double order for you."

"Gus, why do you do what you do?"

"What do you mean Shirley?"

"Why do you always find those sluts who cheat on their husbands to make your deliveries? You do know I am always here, and the girls always welcome you and your services."

"It is because I cannot afford you all."

"Gus, it is always free to deliver to me. Why don't you just settle in with me?"

"Well…"

"Look, I can give as many different panties to you as possible and I promise they will be freshly worn."

"I will think about it, Shirley."

"Meanwhile while you are thinking on it, get over here and give me my bonus delivery…"

THE POLICE DEPARTMENT IS STUMPED

"No robbery, no 'milkman'," says Julia.

"Everything appeared to be in order," says Richard.

"He was there!" exclaims Angela.

"Who, what do you mean Angela?" asks Bobbie.

"I took inventory of the panties you planted in my dresser and one pair is missing," says Angela.

"Are you sure, Angela?" asks Julia.

"Yes, as a matter of fact the pair that is missing, I took note of because I loved them. I wish they had been mine. They are the beige lace type which are quite revealing in all of the important areas, as my husband would say."

"Interesting!" exclaims Richard.

"When would have this happened and how?" asks Julia.

"I don't know because there was no sign of break-in and it must have happened in the time when I was here tying ends together. But I was only absent for an hour. When I returned to your home, Angela, there were no signs that anyone had been there," says Richard.

"I feel that if we can find this 'milkman', then the robberies will be revealed. It is just an intuition," says Bobbie.

"Bobbie, are you pregnant again? Every time you have these intuition episodes and they become true, you are pregnant," says Julia.

"Well, we will see if my intuition turns out to be true once we find him, and then we will revisit whether I am pregnant or not," says Bobbie.

"Bobbie are you…?" asks Richard.

"I should be, Mr. 'milkman' yourself!"

"Well, I guess we will leave that conversation right here where it is. I do have any idea. I think I will take a trip down to Dover Street," says Amanda.

"I don't know about that," says Bobbie.

"What, you don't think I will make a good hooker?"

'Well, I…..'

"Richard!" exclaims Bobbie.

"Amanda be careful down there. You know how territorial those girls are down there. They do not take too kindly to new gals in their space," says Julia.

DOVER STREET

"Hey bitch, what you are doing here?"

"Just visiting," says Amanda.

"Hey, it looks like you are dressed for work. We do not like 'ready to work' bitches in our territory. You go find your own territory and it isn't Dover Street!"

"I am looking for the 'milkman'," says Amanda.

"So, you are looking for a delivery? Not here bitch, go find your own 'milkman'."

"What is all the ruckus out here?" asks Shirley.

"This bitch, here, is trying to crash our territory. She wants a delivery by the 'milkman'."

"You want a delivery?" asks Shirley.

"Yes, I want to visit the 'milkman'," says Amanda.

"Why here? I am sure there are others that can service you," says Shirley.

"I heard he sniffs panties before he does it. That really turns me on," says Amanda.

"Well, now, a kinky bitch! Maybe you will fit in on this street after all."

"Look, I am not trying to invade your territory. My pimp threw

56

me out and I am desperate! I haven't had cock in at least a couple of weeks; it seems an eternity," says Amanda.

"My ladies are rather good at that sort of thing. How about it?"

"No, I am not that kind of slut. I want a real man and a real cock. I want him to hit me hard!" exclaims Amanda.

"All right, have it your way! He usually comes around every day or so. You are lucky because he hasn't been down here for a long time and he told me he was going to be here for a couple of weeks," says Shirley.

THE ALERT

"*J*ulia? This is Amanda."

"Hey kiddo, how are you doing? Are you staying safe in that pussy infested street?"

"Yes, Julia. I will be seeing the 'milkman' rather soon. I am sure he is the guy."

"When? You will need back up, Amanda."

"That is the problem Julia, I don't know when he will show up."

"I can send Richard down there to camp out for a while."

"I am sure Richard wouldn't mind that at all…but Bobbie, well that is a totally different story."

"Julia, I believe I can handle it. I have a couple tricks up my sleeve."

"Amanda, I don't like it! I am coming down there to assist."

"You can't Julia. They know you as the Chief. Believe me, I will call you when it is all over."

"Amanda, I don't like this. Please be careful!"

"Julia, I may be a Forensic Examiner, but I went to the Academy; I am a Police Officer too."

"Yes, I know, Amanda. Remember all the things we have been through together, and your sister. You are like a sister to me. Be safe and call me immediately when you have made your move."

THE LAST DELIVERY

"*H*ey sweetheart! Ready for another delivery? The 'milkman' is here!"

"No, Gus, there is a bitch who is desperate for a delivery. You need to save it for her," says Shirley.

"Oh, one of your girls?"

"No, Gus. She just showed up here a couple of days ago. She said her pimp threw her out."

"Does she know how I work, Shirley?"

"Oh, yes. She is kinky as all hell!"

"Where is she?"

"Down in room fourteen. Have fun lover boy!"

"Hello. Who is it?"

"It is the 'milkman'. I understand you are looking for a delivery?"

"Oh, yes. Come in. The door is open," says Amanda.

"Hey honey! What a beautiful bitch you are. Why would your pimp dump you?"

"It doesn't matter! I need some cock and I want it hard. You had better have saved up…"

"Well look. I was told you like kinky?"

"Yes! What do you want from me?" asks Amanda.

"How about you un-buttoning that gown and take your panties off for me."

"Whoa lover boy. You aren't going to see the prize yet. I need some kinky foreplay…"

"Look bitch, just take off your panties and give them to me!"

"All the time we have been talking, I have gotten them pretty wet. I am sure you are a panty sniffer?"

"Oh, honey, you smell like the sweetest pussy I have ever encountered!"

"Come on, you can sniff those later. Let's get it on!" exclaims Amanda.

"OK, lay down over there on the couch or would you rather get it in the backdoor?" asks Gus.

"No, come here into the bedroom. You like what you smelled? I call the shots if you want where that smell came from. No, no…you put your hands up here," says Amanda.

"I am not sure I like this…cuffed…," says Gus.

"Look, I don't want you touching me until I am ready. I am touching you first," states Amanda.

"Ah…ah…," Gus sighs.

"If you want that 'big boy' planted, you will cooperate!" exclaims Amanda.

"Not until you show me what you have down there…," says Gus.

"Ok, we are done!" exclaims Amanda.

"That is not fair! I am stiff and ready…"

"Put your fucking hands up here on the bedstead!" exclaims Amanda.

"Ok, you got what you wanted, now lower that pussy of yours onto me. I am ready for it. I can almost feel the grip in anticipation…"

"OK, buddy, you are under arrest for the assault and rape of at least two women. Anything you say can and will be used in the court of law," says Amanda.

"You are a cop, bitch? You have no proof! You are just a cunt cop..."

~

"Julia, do you copy?"

"Yes Amanda?"

"He is cuffed, and I have read him his rights. Come on in a get him."

DID YOU REALLY DO IT AMANDA?

"*A*manda, please give us all the details how you pulled this off," says Bobbie.

"Yes, Amanda. Did you really do it?" asks Richard.

"Richard! What kind of question is that?" asks Bobbie.

"Well, I…"

"Ok, guys, I will fill you in with all of the details. First of all, I did not 'do' it. He came to my room and asked me to take off my panties and give them to him so he could sniff them to get himself excited."

"You actually gave him your panties you were wearing?" asks Bobbie.

"No way, I was wearing a gown at the time. I had a pair, not mine, purchased new and tucked them in my waist. He insisted I disrobe while he watched, and I told him he wasn't going to get that if he wanted to make his delivery."

"How did a new pair of panties arouse him, Amanda?"

"A trick I learned in my college days, Julia. There is a readily available product that can mimic, well you know…"

"So, then what happened?" asks Bobbie.

"I knew I had him hooked, so I took the lead and told him to lie down on the bed and put his hands up to the bedstead."

62

"He willingly did that for you?" asks Richard.

"No, he protested, but he was so hooked on the panties, he knew he had to give in and follow my instructions if he wanted in with his 'big boy'."

"So, he never saw you…"

"Bobbie, you mean nude or my…? Nope, he never did. There was no way that bastard was going to see any of me!"

"Amanda, that was just miraculous! I am so glad you are OK!" exclaims Julia.

THE HARFORD POLICE DEPARTMENT
GETS A LUCKY BREAK

"*H*ey Chief, you have nothing on me," says Gus.

"I have witnesses. What is your name?" asks Julia.

"I am the 'milkman'!"

"I am not interested in your perversion. What is your name?"

"Look, is there any way I get off easy if I let you in on a secret, sure to help your Department?"

"What is your name? Maybe I can help you," says Julia.

"My name is Gus Robertson."

"You wouldn't happen to be a relation to Andy Robertson the home inspector?"

"Yes, he is my brother. I accompany him on his home inspections just so I can sniff panties."

"If that is the secret, it doesn't do anything for me or my Department."

"Well, I could ask you to..."

"You had better not go there, Mr. Robertson!"

"No, the secret is concerning the robberies I am sure you are aware of?"

"Let me hear it," says Julia.

"First, I want to know what you are going to do for me," says Gus.

"You mean about reducing the rape charges to assault?" asks Julia.

"Yes, reducing it to assault with some consent?"

"Maybe. It depends on what you will do for me," says Julia.

"OK, my brother contracts to the Remington Real Estate Company doing home inspections for their clients. None of their clients are home during the inspection, so my brother takes inventory of all the expensive furnishings and jewelry. You know, their clients are pretty high society and rich."

"Why the taking of inventory?" asks Julia.

'Well, you see, Claire…"

"Claire?" asks Julia.

Yes, Claire is the owner of the Remington Real Estate Company. Claire sets up the robberies. So, you see, the whole robbery ring is centered around Claire and her company."

"What part of the robbery ring are you in?"

"I have nothing to do with the robberies. I just go there to…"

"I know, sniff panties?" asks Julia.

"Yes."

"Bobbie and Richard, please come in her," says Julia.

"Yes, Julia?" asks Bobbie.

"I need you and Richard to go over to the Remington Real Estate Company and pick up the owner, Claire and arrest her for the robberies. After that, go over to the Andy Home Inspection Company and arrest a Mr. Andy Robertson for assisting the robberies."

"Hey, you can't arrest my brother! I will get in real trouble for telling on him! He will kill me!" exclaims Gus.

"Mr. Robertson, you don't have to worry about that where you are going!" exclaims Julia.

"What? What are you talking about?"

"Let's see, assault leading to rape, which is never consensual by the way, is about fifteen to twenty years and a 'stamp' on your forehead for life," says Julia.

"What? …you promised…you promised!"

"Mr. Robertson, I promised you nothing!"

"You lying fucking cunt!"

"Get out of my sight!" exclaims Julia as she slams the door shut to the holding cell.

THE HOME SALE FALLS THROUGH

"*A*manda, I am truly sorry you lost the purchase of the home on 2245 Stafford Street," says Julia.

"Angela are you sure you won't accept your sister's purchase offer?" says Bobbie.

"Well, I love my sister dearly, but I love my home as well. Besides Robert wouldn't sell our home to my sister," says Angela.

"And why is that Angela?" asks Amanda.

"Because he loves your home too much and he would miss visiting you in your home," answers Angela.

"Angela, my kiddos can't wait for your baby to come. My daughters are already fighting who will babysit him or her and little Richie is praying for a boy; he really wants a brother," says Bobbie.

"Well, Bobbie, let's get the hell out of here and don't tell the sitter we are coming home early. Let's work on just that...," says Richard.

"I just knew it was coming," says Julia with a grin on her face.

"Richard, if you don't tell the sitter you are coming home early, how will you and Bobbie...?" asks Amanda.

"That is what they make backseats for…" says Angela.

"Sister! Where did you…?" asks Amanda.

"That is what they make SUV's for…." says Richard.

"Well, have fun you guys. I am just going home and soak in a very warm and soapy bath," says Julia.

"Me too, Julia," says Amanda.

"Angela, what are you going to do?" asks Amanda.

"Well, after all of this talk, I don't know. Maybe Robert can come home early…"

Julia

Bobbie

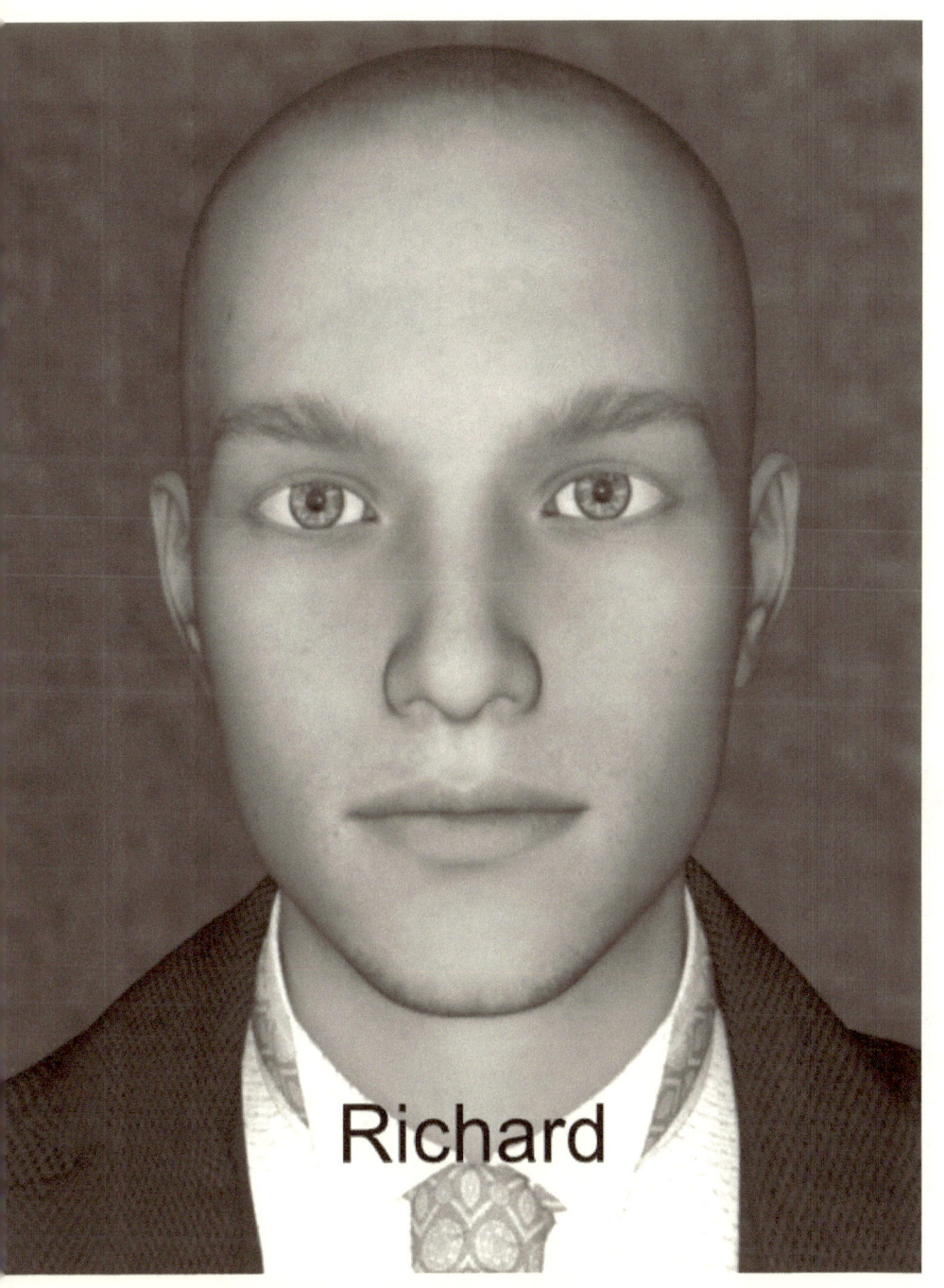

Richard

Amanda

Angela

ABOUT THE AUTHOR

James Roberts is an emerging author who writes stories of crime, suspense, thrillers and romance.

ALSO BY JAMES ROBERTS

A Crisis Of Love And Jealousy

Justice Turns Ugly

Loss To Insanity

The Mortician and The Clown

The Pageant-Georgie Jenks

The Pole Dancer

The Sacrifice For Bobbie

Twisted Personalities

The Sisters

The Breeze That Revealed Her Beauty

An Amish Romance

COVERS TO FOLLOW

A CRISIS OF LOVE AND JEALOUSY

Book One

A Julia Lillus Series

James Roberts

Book One

A CRISIS OF LOVE AND JEALOUSY

James Roberts

Tim draws Julia to his chest and begins to kiss her as
she reaches toward his groin. Immediately there is a
response, and she feels his hardness in her hand. Tim,
then, starts to gently lift Julia's sports bra up over her
breasts.

A story about deceit leading to physical assault.

A romance of erotic sex, physiological devastation, and
murder.

The book draws on reader's emotions and challenges
judgments.

The reader will explore facets of personalities in
characters; formulate opinions based on beliefs and
personal lives.

The Story
Continues......Get
Book Two of the
Series!

9 781736 123416

Justice Turns Ugly

Book Two

A Julia Lillus Series

James Roberts

"Oh, Richard, it was such a great reception after our wedding, wasn't it?" asks Bobbie.
"It sure was, but I have to admit I couldn't wait for it to end so that I could get to know you more....intimately?"
"Oh, Richard, what do you have in mind?"
"Well.....," says Richard.

James Roberts

Publishing

A story about physical assault leading to revenge.

A romance of erotic sex, physiological devastation, and murder.

The book draws on reader's emotions and challenges judgments.

The reader will explore facets of personalities in characters; formulate opinions based on beliefs and personal lives.

The Story Continues...From **Book One** of the Series!

9 781736 123423

LOSS TO INSANITY
JAMES ROBERTS
ANOTHER JULIA LILLUS CRIME THRILLER
LOSS TO INSANITY
James Roberts

Ronald Tier lost his wife to cancer after the birth of his daughter. At the age 10, his daughter is taken from him due to an unfortunate automobile accident. Ron sinks into a deep depressive state and blames the world for his loss. He loses his sense of reasoning and does the unthinkable to get his daughter back.

Police Chief Julia Lillus, again, has her hands full unravelling the case; and to work fast in order to save Amanda from Ron's insanity.

The Mortician And The Clown

James Roberts

Book Three Of A Julia Lillus Series

"Hey, John, congratulations on your new business, and look at that sign, 'Dickerson's Mortuary Services'; very classy!" exclaims Trevor.

"Hell, no! Not her! _____ see she is a real looker, but to be able to get into h_____s. . . fat chance!" exclaims John.

"Hey, Julia, did you hear about the clown at the Syracuse area hospitals?" asks Amanda.
"Yeah, I heard about the clown. Supposedly, the clown, a male, is taking it upon himself to bring joy to the children in the area hospitals."

Cindy begins to dream she is back home in her own bed, but something in her dream doesn't seem right. She sees a faint dark figure walking towards her bed. Suddenly, she feels cold as if the bed coverings were no longer covering her. The dark figure is rubbing her hair and forehead. "Oh, it must be daddy. He always likes to massage my head before I go to sleep," she continues to dream. "Daddy, I love you."

LITTLE DARLINGS

THE PAGEANT

A Julia Lillus Double Crime Thriller

JAMES ROBERTS

"Yeah, what the hell is the matter with mothers?
Entering their girls into pageants and no less
provocative pageants," says Bobbie.
"Yes, they have those little girls dress like teenagers,
makeup and all. They have them wear provocative
clothing and they teach them to move around on stage
in a very suggestive manner," says Amanda.

GEORGIE
JENKS

"Georgie come over here to momma.
I want you to do something for me."
"Do what momma?"
"Come here and I will show you."
"No. momma, I don't want too!"

THE POLE DANCER

ANOTHER JULIA LILLUS
CRIME THRILLER

James Roberts

THE POLE DANCER

James Roberts

JULIA LILLUS AND HER
DEPARTMENT ENTER INTO
A SECRET, BUT DANGEROUS
SCHEME TO SHUT DOWN
THE RING, TO WHERE SHE,
HERSELF, IS PUT DIRECTLY IN
DANGER OF EXPLOITATION.

The Sacrifice For Bobbie

James Roberts

The
Sacrifice For Bobbie

JAMES ROBERTS

"Ah... stop... ah... stop hitting me!"
"I am going to keep hitting you until your entire face is bruised. I want to see blood!"
"How do you know about Ronald Linden?"
"I am his nephew and I promised I would get revenge for you taking his manhood away from him."

CRACK! CRACK! CRACK!

"Ah...ah...why the whip....oh, it is excruciating... stop it!"
"You are going to pay, and this is just the start!"
"What is it you want from me?"
"I want you and then I am going to kill you!"
"What for?"

TWISTED

PERSONALITIES

JAMES
ROBERTS

Mark notices the noise he is hearing becomes a visual of a hobo descending the stairway; at least that is what the figure looks like by the way he/she is dressed. The hobo looks at Mark and smiles while raising his hand in a wave. He skips over to a record player and places a record onto the turntable. As he places the needle onto the record and starts it spinning, the tune "Twinkle, Twinkle Little Star" is heard.

"So what do we have going on Bobble?" asks Julia.
"Well, you see, there was a dead body found in a dumpster on third street over in Hannibal behind a bar. The strange thing is the body was decapitated just like the 'Johnny' case we just unraveled," says Bobbie.
"Interesting! Does the authorities over there want us to intervene?" asks Julia.

Another
Julia Lillus
Crime
Thriller

9 781736 123478

The Sisters

James Roberts

Let me say that I really was not looking for something from her, but if the invitation was put in front of me, I would be tempted to take her up on it. I, being a man of early forties, would be quite delighted to be taken in with such a raven beauty as she.

When she comes to see me at my lounger chair, she has a very seductive smile on her face. I start to tell her my night experiences when she places a finger on my lips as if to hush me. I look at her with question and she whispers to me to see her after lunch in the massage room and I can tell her what I want to tell her then.

9 781736 123447

The Breeze That Revealed Her Beauty

JAMES ROBERTS

"I notice out of the corner of my eye a girl of about twenty years of age walking towards the exit gate of the castle grounds. She has blonde hair, a cute face with just enough makeup to bring her true beauty to fruition. She is wearing a flowing dress colored white and black with flower pastels throughout."

"As I peer into her room, I see a silhouette of her standing in front of the window as the moon shine glows upon her nude body."

"As I look up, her eyes reveal I entered into her intimacy."

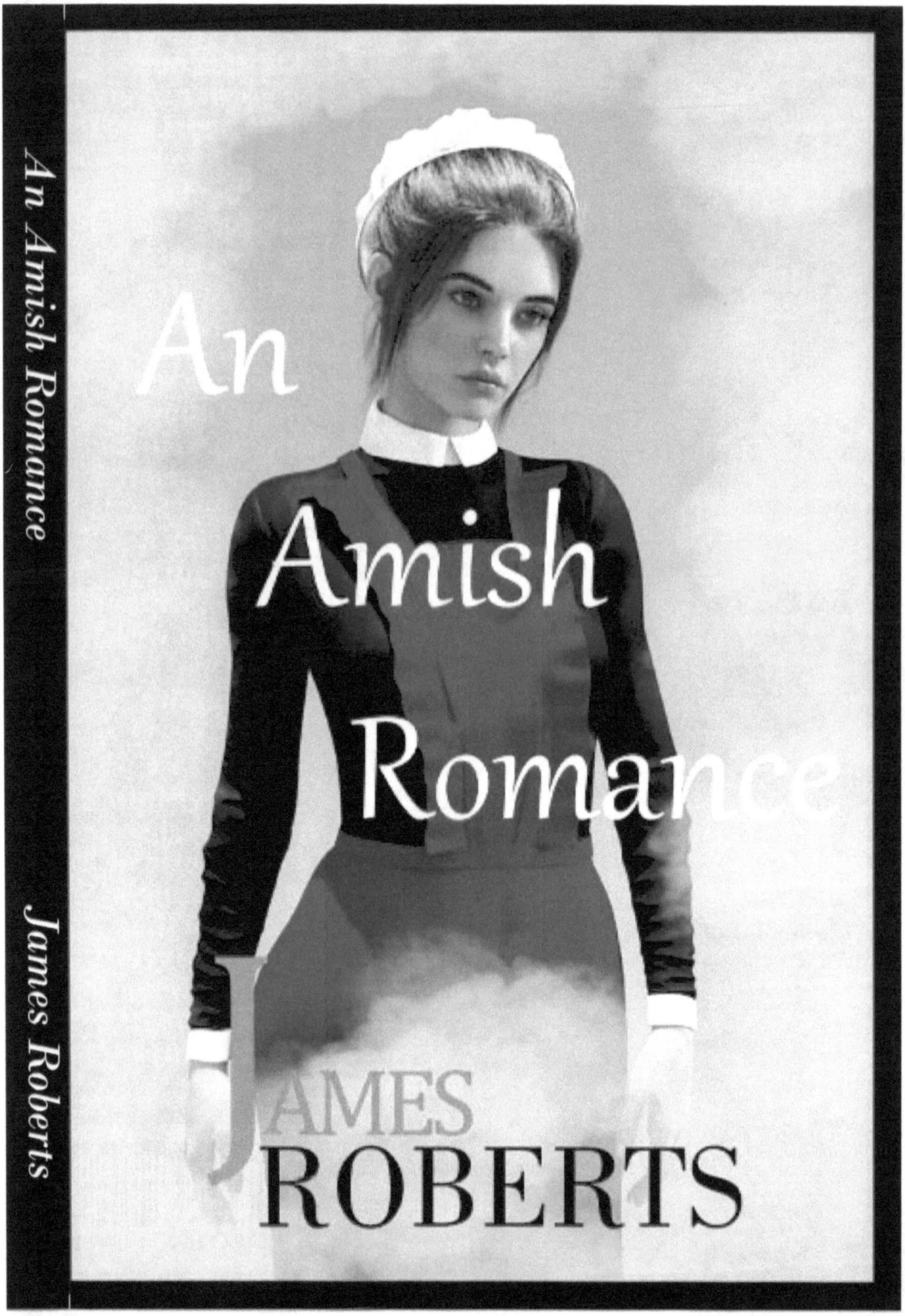
An Amish Romance
James Roberts
An
Amish
Romance
JAMES
ROBERTS

"Paul, I shall not go to your house alone!"

"Delilah, I am just kidding," says Paul as he reaches for Delilah's
hand and lightly places his hand on hers.

"Oh, well, I don't know what to say…Paul?"

"Take my hand, Delilah."

"Paul, I, I, I don't know what to say or do…."

"Say what you feel, Delilah."

"I, I, I, feel kind of strange in my stomach. It is almost like it has
turned upside down."

"Delilah, what if I tell you I am quite fond of you?"

"What does fond mean, Paul?"

"What I am trying to say is I am taking a liking to you, Delilah."

"Well, Paul, I don't know. I, I, never have felt this way before."